FAMILY CIRCUS®

Bil Keane

FAWCETT GOLD MEDAL · NEW YORK

A Fawcett Gold Medal Book
Published by Ballantine Books
Copyright © 1983, 1984 by Cowles Syndicate, Inc.
Copyright © 1988 by King Features Syndicate, Inc.

Library of Congress Catalog Card Numnber: 87-92129

ISBN 0-449-13373-7

Manufactured in the United States of America

First Edition: August 1988

"Mommy says she'll be here in a little bit.
That's sooner than a little while!"

"Is it a rule that you hafta fill up the basket?"

"The big hand is on channel 10, and the little
hand is on channel 3."

"I'm having trouble with eagles in school—one plus one eagles two, two plus two eagles four...."

"Mommy, you have 188 pounds of children!"

"Do we have an eraser that erases crayon?"

"Sure there's a difference between you and me,
Morrie. You're a boy, I'm a girl!"

"I don't WANT to be your little man. I
just want to be a little boy and go
out and play."

"You should always hide your mouth when you cough!"

"Your eyes are very smart, Daddy. They can
read EVERYTHING!"

"Who was the last one in the bathroom?"
"NOT ME." "NOT ME!"

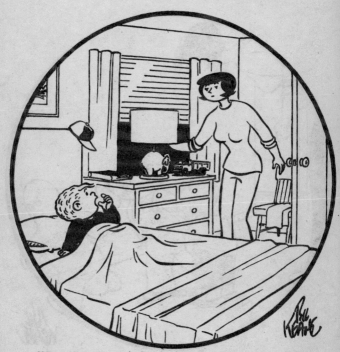

"Don't put out the lights, Mommy. The dark
gets in my eyes and I can't see."

"I opened all the club soda for your party tonight!"

"Shower-curtain rods are not for chinning!"

"Carry me, Mommy? I'm too heavy to walk."

"That white smoke sure is pushin' that plane
real fast!"

"But how can you look up the spelling of a
word if you don't know how to spell it?"

"Poor Mrs. Scott passed away. She was quite old."
"But, you're still quite NEW, aren't you,
Grandma?"

"Daddy, would you put the pretty ones in a
separate pile for me?"

"Promise you won't get mad if I tell
you something?"

"It's wet!"

"The good thing about long hair is you don't hafta wash your neck."

"Dolly, you play the xylophone, Jeffy plays guitar,
PJ plays the drum and I'll play the door chimes!"

"Mommy! Look! Miss Bunn must have run away
from school and she's shoppin' just like a
real person!"

"The party was just gettin' good when we all had
to go home so we wouldn't be in the
firemen's way!"

"Wait right here, Daddy, and hide behind
the tree."

"Can we go around to the houses where nobody
was home last night?"

"PJ did it. He's a real Dr. Juggle and Mr. Hide!"

"Know what's a very pretty
word? Grandmother!"

"Look! Mr. Putz got his name in headlights!"

"I can hardly wait to go to church tomorrow."

"They're havin' a bake sale after!"

"I don't want to go to bed yet, Daddy. Can you stop the clock for awhile?"

"Didn't they have colors when you were a little girl, Grandma?"

"I don't care who does it that way. Put your
shoe and sock back on!"

"Is it OK if I eat some of those little examples
on toothpicks they give out?"

"Look at all those birdies playing
follow-the-leader!"

"I love you, Mommy."
"I love you, too!"
"I love you three!"

"The only good thing about goin' to bed is
you're a day closer to your birthday!"

"It's a soda fountain for soap!"

"Once upon a time...." "You read that one
before, Daddy!"

"Oh, no! The moon's broken again!"

"Grandma's toilet is real pretty! The water is BLUE!"

"Mommy! Look how many tissues fit in this little box!"

"Indoor plants don't get the winter off the way
outdoor plants do!"

"Mommy, would you get this inside-in for me?"

"I guess it won't be going to market today!"

"We learned about the Pilgrims today. They came
to the United States in a Plymouth!"

"This car is a wimp. Let's buy a muscle car, Daddy!"

"Hi, Grandma! Did you come through the woods
and over the river to get here?"

"We just totaled a turkey!"

"Why didn't Santa use his reindeer and sleigh
instead of a helicopter?"

"Where are they taking all those
charcoal briquettes?"

"We hafta go to the bank to buy some money."

"Daddy, how old will you be when I'm
a hundred and fifty?"

"Who's responsible for this old half-eaten
sandwich in the piano bench?"

"Not me."   "Not me."

"Arnold Roth is lucky. His mother's Christmas and his father's Hanukkah."

"Cats wear nails when they want to, but dogs
have them all the time!"

"Did you say POT roast, Mommy? At school they
warned us 'bout using that stuff!"

"In real life Mommy's name is Thel and
Daddy's name is Bill."

"Daddy, who was Pearl Harbor?"

"Hail Mary full of grapes...."

"We don't have timeouts during meals!"

"The Allens have their tree already, and the Flynns have their tree, and the Norquists got theirs, and...."

"What do you want for Christmas?"
"I don't know. What've you got?"

"Mommy baked a whole forest of Christmas trees!"

"Daddy said we shouldn't ask Santa for too many things. I'll chop my list down to a dozen."

"Stop messin' around, Jeffy, and let me
get to sleep!"

"I know what Joseph's first name was. Saint."

"It's OK, Mommy. I won't remember anything
I saw."

"Swaddling clothes are diapers and booties —
stuff like that."

"All you hafta do is go stand under the
mistletoe now when you need a kiss."

"SI-YUL-LENT NIGHT,
HO-OLY NIGHT...."

"Go to sleep, Jeffy. Not a creature's
supposed to be stirring."

"Did everyone in the world get the wrong
sizes for Christmas, Mommy?"

"Santa Claus goofed. He brought Max the helicopter I asked for."

"Mommy! Is Santa Claus still watchin' us
or has he settled down for a long
winter's nap?"

"Look! My sled puts borders on my footprints!"

"Pull down the shade, Mommy, so the dark won't come in!"

"Across from the school? Oh, sure! You're the people who own the horsey and the big black doggy."

"Now we have to go back to January and start
all over again!"

"What's so great? I hate cabbage and I don't like patches!"

"I don't think you have to take ALL your
Christmas presents for Show-and-Tell!"

"Our family is really out of it. We still have a cord on our phone and a pencil sharpener you have to turn."

"It's your move, Mommy!"

"That's why I wanted to shake with my left hand.
I just finished a candy bar."

"It's onion dip, Jeffy. If you want some you use these 'tato chips as shovels."

"My shoelaces keep unwinding!"

"Now that we've got cable, none of these clicks are empty!"

"Guess what?"
"What?"
"That's what!"

"Come on, Mommy! Richard Simmons said to keep exercising while the commercial's on!"

"I like breakfast best 'cause you don't need
many table manners."

"PJ, are you absolutely, positively SURE you
want to go outside?"

"We're all gonna be fingerprinted at school. Do you think they'll take mug shots too?"

"Look what I can do, Grandma!"

"We don't have a ladies' room at school. It's
a girls' room!"

"Grandma! Your TV gets the same shows as our TV!"

"I sure hope Snow White doesn't eat the poison apple this time!"

"Which are we gonna get next, Mommy? Another
baby or another animal?"

"Look at Barfy! He's got dog food on his nose!"

"Eeny, meeny, miny, mo. . . ."

"I don't want to be Mo!"

"Claire swallowed a button and they're takin' her
to the hospital to have her X-rated!"

"I'll always love you, Grandma. Even when I'm a hundred!"

"When will the carpet cleaners be finished?"

"Couldn't I just carry my lunch in an old brown paper bag?"

"My doll has a birth certificate and
'doption papers."

"That's nothin'! Mine has a driver's license!"

"If that's a new moon what happened to the old one?"

"Can I have that skirt when you outgrow it, Mommy?"

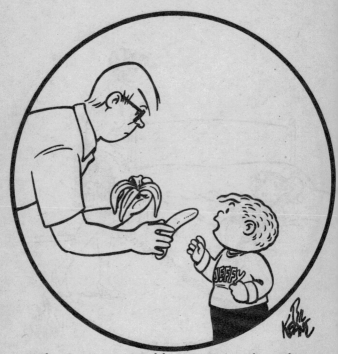

"That's wrong, Daddy. Mommy only undresses
it halfway!"

"Don't scream at me, Dolly! I'm not death, y'know."

"The sound's better if you dribble in the kitchen."

"Want me to get on your back?"

"Jon Kurtz asked his mom to get him a used dog. They can't afford a new one."

"Grandma can do lots of things around the house.
She learned them from Mommy!"

"Does it bovver you when people keep askin'
questions, Daddy? Does it, Daddy?
Daddy?..."

"And if Cupid shoots you with his arrow, you're in love whether you like it or not!"

"Dolly keeps takin' her heart pills and won't give me some."

"You may each have one more before I transplant
this heart to a safer place!"

"I'd offer you a chocolate if I could remember
where I hid them from the kids."

"How old do I hafta be to change my name from Billy to Bill?"

"You've let it ring long enough!"
"Wait. I think I hear someone coming!"

"Can I have a bite to eat while you're making my sandwich?"

"The record player has the hiccups and keeps sayin'
the same thing over and over."